StumpHouse Stories

For Phoebe, the littlest of them all

Howard M. Stien

Pictures by Christina Hogue

Phoebe and the Bare Bear

Once upon a year, not so long ago, there was a little girl whose name was Phoebe. Phoebe was four years old. She lived with her Mom and Dad and her brothers and sister. And Phoebe was the littlest of them all.

Phoebe liked to play outdoors where she could run and swing and hide and find flowers. Best of all she liked to sleep outdoors in the tent.

But sometimes she didn't get to sleep outdoors in the tent because she was the littlest of them all. When Phoebe slept in the tent someone had to sleep with her. "That's so you won't be afraid," her Mom said.

"I won't be afraid," Phoebe told her Mom.

"Wait until you grow some more. And when you are bigger you can sleep alone in the tent," her Mom said.

"I wish I could go to Gramom's house. She lets me do everything I want even though I am the littlest of them all. When I go to Gramom's house she will let me sleep outdoors all by myself," Phoebe said.

Phoebe did go to Gramom's house. But she couldn't sleep outdoors in the tent because Grandad and Gramom didn't have a tent. They had something that was better than a tent. It was a tree house. A tree house is a little house up in a tall tree.

Only this tree house wasn't up in a tall tree. It was built on the top of a stump. Now, a stump is a tree with its top cut off.

"The top of a stump is a good place to build a play house," Grandad said. "It's a Stump House."

"I am going to sleep in the Stump House all by myself," Phoebe said. She told Gramom she wouldn't be afraid. "The animals are my friends," she said.

So after dinner and when it was getting dark, Phoebe went to sleep in the Stump House. She took her sleeping bag with her. That was so she would stay warm. She took some cookies with her. That was so she wouldn't get hungry.

And so she wouldn't be lonely she took her teddy bear with her. His name was Barely Bear. He wasn't a very big bear. Sometimes Phoebe called him Barely, but most of the time she called him Bare. That was his nickname. And sometimes she just called him Bear.

She took Grandad's flashlight with her. That was so she could see if there was something she wanted to see.

Phoebe crawled into the sleeping bag. She pulled Barely Bear close to her. She ate a cookie and played with the flashlight. This is fun she thought. I am sleeping outdoors all by myself even though I am the

littlest of them all. Finally, she closed her eyes and fell fast asleep hugging Barely Bear.

After she had been sleeping for awhile, Phoebe thought she heard someone knocking on the door. She listened and listened again. It wasn't someone knocking on the door. Someone was scratching on the window.

Phoebe shined her flashlight on the window. And what do you think she saw looking in the Stump House window?

There was a big, bare bear. He didn't have his fur coat on and he was cold without his coat.

When the bare bear saw Phoebe's light he said, "May I come in? I am so cold."

Now this was a big, bare bear and the Stump House door was small. It was made for children, not big, bare bears. Phoebe felt sorry for the big, bare, cold bear. But she couldn't let him come in. Gramom had said, "Don't let any strangers come into the Stump House." And this was the strangest bear she had ever seen. Besides, he was too big for the door.

"You can't come in. The door is too small. And I can't let strangers come in the Stump House when I am all alone," Phoebe said.

"I am very cold," the big bare bear said. And he started to cry.

That surprised Phoebe because she didn't know that bears could cry. "What happened to your coat?" Phoebe asked the big, bare bear.

"I washed it and hung it on a tree to dry. And somebody took it while I was napping," said the bear.

"I know what I will do," Phoebe said to herself. "I will help him find his coat."

Phoebe ate another cookie and then she took her flashlight and slipped out of the Stump House. She told the bear to come with her and not to make any noise.

"Be quiet. We don't want to wake Gramom. She told me not to talk to strangers," Phoebe said.

Phoebe and the bear walked very quietly to the neighbor's house. They looked in the window and there on the floor by the fireplace was the bare bear's coat.

The neighbors had made
a rug out of the bear's coat.
Phoebe opened the window
and the big bare bear
reached in with his long
arm and pulled his coat
out by the leg. He tried
it on and it fit just right.

"I know it is mine," he
whispered. "It's so
warm and it feels
so good." He wasn't
cold anymore and he
wasn't bare either.

"Thank you," the big bear said.

He gave Phoebe a big, bear hug. It wasn't a big, bare, bear hug. It was only a big, bear hug because they had found his coat and he was wearing it. Then he walked off into the woods.

Phoebe didn't go back into the Stump House. She sat on the steps and thought about the big bear who wasn't a bare bear anymore. Then she and Barely Bear went into Gramom's house to tell her about their dream.

There were a lot of days in the summer Phoebe was four. On one of those days she was at Gramom's house. It was Grandad's house too, but Phoebe just called it Gramom's house. It took too much time to say Gramom's and Grandad's house.

When the summer nights were warm Phoebe would sleep in Grandad's Stump House. It was Gramom's Stump House too, but Phoebe only called it Grandad's Stump House because he had built it for Phoebe to play in.

One of those summer days when Phoebe was four she went to sleep in the Stump House all by herself, even though she was the littlest of them all. She took a blanket with her so she could cover her head if she heard something that made her afraid. She took some cookies with her. And she took some milk in a glass.

"You have to have milk when you eat cookies," Phoebe told Gramom.

The night was warm and the moon was bright.

"I like sleeping in my Stump House when it's warm and the moon is bright," Phoebe said to herself (because nobody else was there).

She ate one of her cookies and saved one to eat if she woke up hungry. She drank some milk but saved some for the other cookie. Then she pulled her blanket over her head (just in case) and went to sleep.

When she woke the sun was shining and the birds were singing. She wanted to sleep some more but the early birds were singing so loudly that she couldn't go back to sleep. "I am going to eat my other cookie," Phoebe said to herself (because nobody else was there).

She pulled off her blanket, sat up and reached for her cookie. It was gone. Her milk was gone too, but there were some cookie crumbs in the bottom of the glass.

Who ate my cookie and drank my milk, Phoebe wondered. And why are there cookie crumbs in my glass? It can't be my brother because he didn't come to Gramom's House.

All day Phoebe wondered about her missing cookie. Maybe it was Marmalade, the neighbor's black and orange cat, she thought. "But cats can't put cookie crumbs in a glass," she told Gramom.

The next night Phoebe had a plan. "If the night is warm and the moon is bright, I will sleep in the Stump House," she said to Gramom. "I will only pretend to sleep. Then if somebody comes to steal my cookie, I will catch him. And I will tell him it's not nice to take someone's cookie when she is sleeping."

The night was warm and the moon was bright, and Phoebe went to sleep in her Stump House. She took a blanket with her so she could cover her head, if she heard something that made her afraid. She took some cookies with her. And she took some milk in a glass.

She ate one of her cookies and saved one to catch the cookie thief. She drank some milk but saved some to see who was putting crumbs in her glass.

Phoebe pulled her blanket over her head and pretended to sleep. Pretending to sleep when you are tired is not easy. And even though she tried hard not to, Phoebe fell sound asleep.

After she had been sleeping for awhile, Phoebe was wakened by a lot of noise. Somebody was in the Stump House. She kept the blanket over her head and listened. Who is making all that racket she wondered. Slowly and quietly she peeked out from under her blanket.

A big raccoon was holding her cookie and singing: "Look what I've found! A cookie! A cookie I've found."

Then he took the cookie and dunked it in the milk Phoebe had saved. "Oh no! It all fell apart again," he cried loudly. He had held the cookie in the milk too long.

Phoebe threw off her blanket and said, "Who are you? Why are you making all this racket? And why are you stealing my cookie?"

"My name is Ruckus. I am making all this racket because my cookies always crumble."

"Those were my cookies," Phoebe said. "Why are you stealing them?"

"Raccoons don't steal food. They find it. I found the cookies and I didn't know they were yours. I am sorry. I promise I won't take your cookies again. Besides, cookies aren't good raccoon food. We always wash food before we eat it and you can't wash cookies."

Now Phoebe knew who had been taking her cookies and why the crumbs were in her glass. "That was my cookie," Phoebe said, "and it was you who stole my cookie last night."

"I didn't steal your cookie. I took it. Don't you know the difference? Besides, I won't take any more of your cookies. They are not good raccoon food. Crayfish are better because they don't crumble when you wash them. Have you ever seen a crumbled crayfish?" Ruckus asked.

Before Phoebe could say that she had not even seen an uncrumbled crayfish, Ruckus left to go to the pond to find some crayfish.

The next thing Phoebe heard was, "Breakfast is ready, Phoebe. Are you hungry?"

Phoebe was quiet while she ate her breakfast. "What are you thinking about?" Gramom asked.

"I was thinking about the raccoon," she said.Then she told Gramom about the raccoon named Ruckus.

"That Stump House sure makes you imagine things," Gramom said, "Maybe you should keep the door closed when you sleep out there."

Phoebe and Porky the Porcupine

Most of the time Phoebe lived with her Mom and Dad and her brothers and sister. Sometimes she stayed at her Gramom's house. Her brothers and sister went to school, but Phoebe didn't go to school because she was the littlest of them all. She was only four years old and you have to be five before you can go to school.

"I wish I could go to school," Phoebe said to her Mom. "I don't ever get to go anywhere. It's because I am the littlest of us all."

"You should go to Gramom's house. You could stay there for awhile," said her Mom, "You could play in the Stump House."

"Even if I am the littlest of us all?" Phoebe asked.

"Even if you are the littlest of us all," said her Mom.

When Phoebe got to Gramom's house summer was over. The leaves had fallen from the trees and it was getting colder every day. Then it started to snow, so Phoebe didn't play in the

Stump House after that. "It's too cold to play out in the Stump House," she told Gramom.

One morning Grandad looked out the window and saw that the Stump House door was open.

"Why is the Stump House door open?" he asked Gramom. "It should be closed so the animals won't go inside and make a mess in there."

"What animals?" Gramom said. "There aren't any animals who would want to be in the Stump House."

"I saw some squirrels looking in the door one day and a chipmunk was on the steps yesterday," Grandad said.

"But did you see them inside the Stump House?" Gramom asked.

"No, but I bet they go in there when we are not looking. I smelled a skunk out there one day. And another day, I saw a coyote sniffing around the hillside. Phoebe, please go out there, close the door and lock it so none of those animals can get in. I think they all may be looking for a place to sleep during the winter when it's cold," Grandad said.

Phoebe put on her warm coat and went out to the Stump House. But before she closed the door

she looked in to see if any animals were inside. Then she heard somebody say in a very prickly voice, "Don't you knock before you poke your nose into somebody's house?"

There in the Stump House doorway was a big prickly porcupine. And he was talking to Phoebe.

"This is our house now," the porcupine said. "We waited until that little girl stopped playing in here. Then we moved in and we are going to stay all winter. There is a big woodpile close by so we will have plenty of food when the snow covers the ground."

"PLEASE don't close the door because we can't get it open. We were going to stay here last year but the ice storm froze the door shut and we couldn't get it open. We were so glad when that little girl who plays here sometimes left the door open. Are you that little girl?"

Phoebe looked in the window of the Stump House.
She had to look in the window because the big
prickly porcupine was standing in the doorway
and she didn't want to get stickered by his quills.

And this is what Phoebe saw.

In one corner there was a big pile of leaves from the lilac bush and all snuggled in the pile of leaves was a mother porcupine and a little porcupine. They were sound asleep.

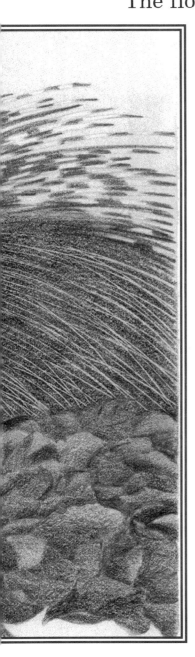

The floor had a thick carpet of pine needles and in another corner was a stack of twigs and bark, which is what porcupines eat. The Stump House was cozy and warm.

But the porcupine wanted to talk. He said that soon he had to go to sleep for the long winter, because that is what all porcupines do after they find a nice warm, dry place to stay.

"Nobody is supposed to talk during the Big Sleep and keep the others awake, but I am not sleepy yet. My name is Porky. My wife's name is Portense and our little one's name is Potpourri," he said. "What is your name? Do you eat bark too? Do you sleep all winter?" the porcupine asked.

Just as Phoebe was going to tell him that she couldn't imagine sleeping all winter, Gramom called from the deck, "You better come in now, Phoebe. It's time to rest for awhile."

While Phoebe rested she fell asleep. When she woke up she told Gramom about the porcupines in the Stump House.

"There aren't any porcupines in the Stump House. You must have dreamed that," Gramom said.

"Well, what is this?" Phoebe asked.

"Oh my! It looks like a porcupine quill. Where did you get it?" Gramom asked.

"When I went to close the Stump House door, it stuck to my sleeve." Phoebe said,

Phoebe was quiet for awhile and then she asked, "Do you think Porky and his family will really sleep in the Stump House all winter long?"

Phoebe and Roma the Skunk

Phoebe woke up early. The sun was just coming up and the birds were singing their morning songs. Then she remembered she had been sleeping in the Stump House. The birds always woke her when she slept in the Stump House.

She wondered why the birds always woke up before everybody. Maybe it was because they are early birds, she thought.

"They are early birds." Grandad had said that when Phoebe asked him what kind of birds they were.

"I like waking up in the Stump House," Phoebe said to herself (because no one was up except the birds).

Usually the air was cool and smelled fresh. Phoebe would pull her blanket close and think about what she was going to do all day. But today the air in the Stump House smelled bad. Even pulling her blanket over her head couldn't make the smell go away.

Phoebe pulled off her blanket so she could go into the big house. Then she saw something sleeping in the corner. It was all rolled up into a black and white furry ball.

When Phoebe sat up the furry ball woke up, stretched, and said, "Good morning." And when it moved the bad smell seemed to get worse.

"Who are you? Are you making my Stump House smell bad?" Phoebe asked.

"My name is Roma. I don't think your house smells bad. It smells like me," she said.

"Why do you smell like that?" Phoebe asked.

"I am a skunk. We don't smell like this all the time, only when we are scared," the little skunk said.

"Are you scared now?" Phoebe asked.

"No, but I was last night. My mother and my sister and I were hunting slugs and bugs to eat like we do every night. And a big dog tried to catch us. Your door was open and I came in here to hide. I must have fallen asleep." Roma said.

"Why does it smell bad, if you aren't scared now?" Phoebe asked.

"I am just learning and got in the way," the little skunk said.

"Learning what?" Phoebe wanted to know.

"Learning to squirt. We squirt dogs and cats and things that scare us. We can't smell it but other animals can and they leave us alone. Do you think I smell bad?"

"Yes, I do and it isn't nice. You should learn how to stay out of the way or you will never have any friends," Phoebe said.

Just then Phoebe heard a dog bark. Roma heard it too and up went her tail. Without saying goodbye and with her tail high she hurried off into the woods.

Roma is scared again, Phoebe thought. The air was beginning to smell bad.

"Phoebe, it's time for breakfast," Gramom called.

While Phoebe was eating breakfast she said,
"I have to remember to close the Stump House
door before I go to sleep."

Then she told Gramom about Roma, the skunk.

Most of the time Gramom thought Phoebe was
imagining when she told about the animals who
came to the Stump House.

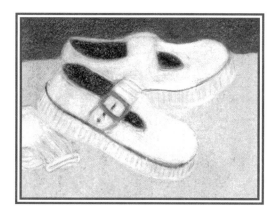

But today Gramom really believed her.